CHAOS

THE SILENT WAR

SIDRAT WANI

Contents

Foreword

The author has started the book with the line that "she was going to be 19 in an hour, as it was 11 PM , 29 November"
The author started the day with praying and thanking Allah for the things He has given her and the things he took away from her which were hurting her. She is thankful for each person who walked in and out in her life.
The author started to clean her room and she found her shelves are filled with art projects and she wanted to keep them even if they turn ugly. While cleaning the room her eyes fell on a dusty box and she found many things in it. She opened the box in a dramatic way and found many things in it like friendship band, bead in a string, envelope of old wedding, two key chains in the envelope, benten toy and birthday card that she had made for her Aapi.
The author says that she hate clocks as the tick tick sound creeps her out. She never wants to sleep with the clock ticking in her room.
The author has lost her father in a very young age. She doesn't even remember him. Her mother had told her that Abu had been out for job she was then three years old and it was difficult for author to understand what was going. But one day her sister told her the real truth about her Abu. The author has lost her maamu, naanu and dadi as well. The truth is that there is always a void in her heart in their place. My orbs are filled with tears that author used to thought that sky would become heavy one day with people and it would no longer hold people and give them back to us.
The author says it was july 2012 when she got to know about the meningitis. She was lucky that she was hospitalized in time otherwise it could have been life

threatening. In the hospital she was missing her empty house, it's walls and lawn too. The author has mentioned "Maasi" here who used to teach her Quran and the author has burst into tears before her. Maasi had bought her drawing books and some colours. From then onwards author got obsessed with drawing. Those colours filled her stressed colourless life.

While writing the forward of book i am literally crying as it is not easy for anyone to loose her father. Seeing her friends with their fathers is tearful scene for her. When she goes to places and sees friends with her fathers. She smiles and to them she is happy. But on the inside she is sad. She is screaming out to them so that they might see she is not doing as okay as they think. Everytime she tries to make someone understand that she is alone or she needs help. They are blinded by her plastered smile or they go deaf be her loud calling. Don't she deserve the love of her father? Don't she deserve the open arms of her father? Oh God! this system of death is very cruel.

I am myself complaining to God why is her pain never ending. Is she different from the rest. She is tired of searching the peace. God why you have chosen to forsake her? Haven't you punished her enough? She cry herself to sleep every night and day hoping, praying that you hear her. Lord she is tired of being tired. Lord hear her hear her cries. She is tired.

The author has ended the book by mentioning about her panic attacks. The author seems to be ready for crying but pretending to be brave. She hates the person she has become. She is not ready to smile again. The death of her loved ones has crushed her heart. The pieces are still on her hand and the scars are still there from where it cut her.

For the author writing feels like untangling all her chaos.

Chaos is her favourite word so is the name of book.
Dear Author I only say this " Let's weather the storm and meet on the other side "
    RIZWAN MUSHTAQ RATHER
    AUTHOR OF THREE BOOKS

Preface

"You know your soul is dead when pick up your pen and don't feel storms inside you"
Writing is the greatest gift God has given me. Writing is the outlet for all my worries and stress. I am thankful to those who supported me throughout this journey.
There a lot of things that one doesn't talk about. There are some feelings that we choose to not talk about but there is only so much a person can hold inside. I held it inside for years. Now is the time that I let it go. i wrote this book as a sign of leaving all that behind me.
You never know what a person has been through and what impact that has had on them. In this book, I have tried to explain some complex emotions that we feel but never talk about.

Acknowledgements

Sidrat Wani, born in 2003, is a medical student and an aspiring doctor from Tral. Obsessed with literature from her childhood, Sidrat began penning her thoughts on paper since 5th grade. She is a poet as well as a proser who usually likes to write about teenage and youth.

She commenced her schooling from F.V.M.S. Tral where she discovered her immense love for literature. She was recognized by most of the students as a multitalented artist and had an exceptionally good reputation among her schoolmates because of her writing and art. She graduated from the school in 2020 and started her journey as a medical student.

She has composed a number of poems and proses throughout her years as a high school student. Apart from being an artist and a writer, Sidrat is also very good at photography and often posts on social media. Sidrat also has a strong affection towards nature, the proofs of which can be seen in art and photography.

CHAPTER ONE

"Some wars are meant to be fought in silence"

CHAPTER TWO

Dear reader,

Life doesn't always go as you planned. People always say that everything happens for a reason but I don't believe that. I believe that when anything bad happens we just attach it everything that happens after it . if anything good happens after it, we say that might have happened for a reason. But if anything bad happens, we say that it's just our bad luck.

Everyone knows that sadness and grief is a test from Allah but we always forget that happiness is the real test. In sadness we turn to Allah but we never thank Him for our happiness.

So be thankful for what we you have. Appreciate every moment that you get to live your loved ones.

CHAPTER THREE

"She was left alone in the aches
She could hear her breath,
Screaming her defeat.
Her heart was bruised and cold
Her tears fuelled her soul
As it kept burning
She kept crying for help
But all she could hear back was silence
A never-ending silence
And one day her voice echoed across the emptiness
She realized she the only one
Who hear her screams
Who could calm her chaos
She wrapped her arms around herself
And hugged herself so tightly
That all the broken pieces of her came together
So her love for herself become her sword
One by one she conquered all her wars
And established peace
She was warrior, fighting for herself"

CHAPTER FOUR

"She couldn't face the light,
Consumed by the darkness within her,
Her soul was anchored to the darkest harbors,
Across the oceans of fear;
With the chaos she immersed deep deep down,
With her heart turned to stone,
Surrounded by her demons,
With no swords, no shields,
She sailed into the darkness,
In the darkness she saw pieces of herself,
That she left behind with each step,
There was no storm she didn't fight,
She saw the warrior she once was,
Proudly she set her soul free
And let in the light through every inch of her skin"

CHAPTER FIVE

Its 11PM, 29th of November. I'm going to be 19 in an hour. My mother always used to say that you are a kid till you are 18. I never understood what she meant by "being a kid". I thought maybe it meant that you were free to make mistakes and learn, which are both very different things. We put so much pressure on our mistakes to teach us something but we need to understand that they might just be moments where we simply messed up. Now that I am leaving these 18 years behind me I have started to understand what she meant. Being a kid is just like getting our default settings. Now don't get me wrong, you might think that there a lot of things that we learn when we grow up but I believe we have already learned everything as kids but it needs to be modified time to time. Today was very important for me because today I went down the memory lane and there was a lot a got to know about myself. I won't say that I have done anything great these 18 years but I don't think I wasted it. I have had my fair share of good and bad experiences and that's made me who I am today.

I started the day with praying and thanking Allah for things He has given me and the things He took from me which were hurting me. I am thankful for each person who walked in and out of my life. I am thankful for each blessing which He sent and each pain that kept me grounded. There was a lot inside my heart. There was a never ending chaos which could drown anyone but I had chained my heart and hid its key under the deepest ocean. But today I decided to let it go because jumping into the chaos was the only way for me to check its depth.

So after I prayed I decided to clean my room. I have this habit of reorganizing my room after every measure change in my life or just after exams to just leave that atmosphere of stress behind. Today was a major day so I decided to deep clean my room, like really cleaning its soul. I knew I was going to be distracted by seeing the things in my drawers which I haven't used in a while but it was not going to bother me today. I had it in my mind that I wanted to revisit every part of me today. Cleaning my room is a very hectic process because I am a very messy person. I had to meet my friends later so I had to finish this quickly.

I started by cleaning the shelves and let me tell you this I had never been the kind of kid who would have trophies on their shelves. My shelves were filled with art projects which most of the people found ugly but I had kept each one of them because it was hard for me to let go of things that I put so much effort into. I would still keep them even if they turned ugly. The only thing worth being on display on my shelves was the school group photo. The feeling of looking at that photo has still not changed. I was still embarrassed by the fact that I was the only girl not wearing leggings. I still remember how the photographer yelled at one of my friends because she didn't know what to do with her hands while posing for the photo. I can still clearly see through that photo how hard she was trying to control her tears. Seeing that photo reminded me of how scared I was to grow up. I remember when my first tooth was about to fall. I was at school, crying in the washroom when one of my seniors came. She was my neighbor and she is the sweetest person

I have met till date she used to love all the kids so much. Everyone used to call her gudiya.She came up to me and asked me what was wrong. I said "my tooth is gonna fall, if I tell mama she is going to take me the dentist and I'm scared of the dentist. You need to call Aapi right now" the dentist was one of my friend's father and I remember the teachers used to tell him you must have a castle build out of peoples teeth. That visual is still as uncomfortable as it was that time. While I was crying she started to laugh and said "this is just a sign of growing up" and I remember I started to cry even harder because I was so afraid of growing up.

After cleaning the shelves I looked at the clock that did not work because I had removed its cells. I have always hated clocks, there's something about the way they sound that creeps me out. I could never sleep with a clock ticking in my room. Then I cleaned the clock. After that I thought of moving my bed .I can't be the only one who has a random shoe box under her bed in which I have kept things that remind me of the people I love. I saw that box from a distance, I remember I had put a little bow on it but it was gone and the box was covered in dust because I had not put anything in it for a while. I took the box and I dusted it off. As soon as I opened it, a spider crawled out of it and I dropped the box. I had planned to open that box in a dramatic way and take the things out one by one but there I was. Now I had to pick everything up and put it back in that old dusty box and I had to figure out where the spider disappeared that I saw few second ago. It could be hanging on my clothes, it could be climbing on the bed, it could be anywhere. Normally I wouldn't sit in peace until I got the spider out of my room but I was more curious about seeing what was in the box. The first thing that caught my eye was a friendship band which was torn and I had made a little bow out of it now I don't remember who gave me that but it must have been important to me. The next thing I found was a bead in a string. I exactly remember how it got there. I had once broken a button of my shirt when I was little so I went to my grandma so she could sew it back. She pulled out that box that had always disappointed me. It was a candy box with threads and needles in it. I would always think there was candy in it but then I would open it and tell myself that I would never fall for this again but did every time I saw that box. I think that is where I got my trust issues from. That day when I opened it, I saw a pretty little bead in it; it was a bead from her tasbeeh. I liked it so much so she let me keep it. It looked somewhat like marble. Its sapphire blue color is still as pretty to me as it was that day because how can you love something one day and the next day you decide it is not important.

The next I found was an envelope of an old wedding invitation which for a change was not addressed to my father with 'late' written in front of his name. Inside it was a piece of paper with a song written in it which my mother used to sing to me when I was little. The song was called "pappa jaldi aaja na" it went like

saat samundar paar se, gugiyon ke bazaar se

From a doll store across the seven seas,

achhii sii gugiyaa laanaa

Please bring us back a doll.

gudiyaa chaahe na laanaa, pappaa jaldii aajaa na!

Whether you bring a doll or not, please come home soon, Papa!

I didn't understand that before but as I grew up I began to understand how deep it was. I used ask my mother "Why doesn't Abu come back now?"

My mother had told me that Abu had been out for his job.

For a three years old child it was difficult to understand the meaning of death. My grandma used to tell me that Abu will come back when I grow up. Growing up with the hope that day I'll meet my Abu wasn't easy. There was so much chaos in my head. For years I believed that he would come back and we could like a normal family just like my friends do. Then one day my sister told me "they are fooling you. They are lying to you. Abu is never going to come back. God has taken him away from us. He is gone". That didn't make sense to me at that time. I used to look at the sky believing that Abu was somewhere in there. I used to think "how far has God kept Abu?" I thought one day the sky would become heavy by people, it would no longer hold people and give them back to us. I wouldn't even remember how Abu looked if we didn't have photographs of him. I used to look at his photo with my eyes filled with tears and I would ask him "why didn't you spend time with me? Three years were not enough for me. You didn't like me, right? That's why you ran away from me" I used to complain to God "why isn't my dad with me? All of my friends talk about their dads, didn't I deserve it? I used think it was my fault. My mom used to tell me how Abu stayed up nights to cradle me to sleep when I cried. As a child I thought he was annoyed by me which was the reason he left.

I also found two key chains in the envelope one with Abu's name written on it and another one was like a little wallet with a five rupee coin in it. My mom used to say when my father got home from work; he used to give all the change to my cousin who was very young at that time. My mother always told me that it was stupid of me to save that coin but whenever I looked at that coin, I always wondered what my would do with it. There must have a reason that he kept that coin.

The next thing that I found was a ben10 toy. God I hated Ben10 so much. I never got it. My childhood best friend used to make me watch it. Well he didn't make me watch it but I used be at his house all the time so I had to watch it. His dad was my teacher. He was the one who made me understand what learning was not about remembering things, it was about understanding. Well the story of that toy is a very long one.

"It was July, 2012. I was lying in bed, cry out of pain. My whole body ached. I felt like my head was going to burst out of pain. I used to walk on my toes because my heals would hurt. I was rushed to the doctor in the nearby clinic. It was the doctor I had been visiting since I was little. He was the kind of doctor no kid would be scared of especially me because whenever I went to him, he would always send me back with gifts or candies. I expected the same this time but he suggested that I should be taken to the hospital. I thought it would be just a regular checkup. They did some tests and I was admitted there. We got to know that I had meningitis, an inflammation in the (meninges) membranes that surround our brain and spinal cord. The doctors said I was lucky that I was taken to the hospital in time otherwise it could have been life threatening.

My mom told me "you are lucky that you are lucky that you're born in this modern era. We didn't have treatment for these diseases in the past. People would die because of meningitis in the past"

"PEOPLE USED TO DIE"

That was all that hovered in my mind. When we reached the hospital, my uncle bought me that Ben10 toy. I really thought I was going to die. For the first few days I cried a lot. I wanted to go home. I didn't want to die in the hospital. I just thought that if I am dying, I want to die at home. The doctors used to ask me "your whole family is here, what do you miss now?" I said "I even miss the empty house, I miss its walls and the lawn too," they would laugh at it but only I knew what was going on in my head. Then one day one of my friend's mom came. She used to teach us Quran. We call her "maasi" but she is much more than that. I could hide my tears from anyone but not her. Even today when she asks me what is wrong, I just burst into tears. Everyone used to buy me toys but I never played with them but she bought me a drawing book and some colors. From then onwards I got obsessed with drawing. I forgot about all the pain and I just kept drawing and coloring all the day. The doctors were confused because now I didn't say a word about going back home. Those colors actually filled my stressed colorless life. When I was discharged from there I had to give all of those toys to the other kids who were still in the hospital because my mom didn't want any memories of this experience but somehow my mom had packed that Ben10 toy with the other stuff. I didn't want any memory of that horrible place either but now that I think about, these experiences are so important. Us humans, we do everything to get peace. Peace is just like the candy that we give a kid after we make them eat that they didn't want to eat and they are happy about it only until it's in the wrapper. When they're like wow we have a candy. The reality hits when it's out of the wrapper and they know they only taste if they're ready for it to disappear after a while. I have realized this one because I've been around a lot of kids. Remember there used to be those lollypops with the chewing gum in the center? The most tasteless chewing gums. As kids we used to be excited about THAT chewing gum when it wasn't even the most enjoyable part. It didn't even taste good I don't think it tasted like anything .We used to forget to enjoy the actual lollypop because of the chewing gum just because it was hidden. We always keep our eyes on the destiny and never enjoy the journey.

The next thing was a birthday card that I had made for Aapi. One day I found it crumpled under her books. She didn't treat it the way she was supposed to, so I took it back. I how remember disappointed I was at that time. She has been one of best friends and as a kid, seeing that card like that felt like betrayal. Well she has been important part of life because she has saved my life twice by saving me from two accidents. The first time was when we were once walking on the road and a car was approaching right towards us and it was fast that I didn't think that I could move fast enough to get out of its way but Aapi pushed me out of the way and she got hit by the car and broke her arm. I hadn't cleaned my room at all and it was already 2PM so freshened up, I opened my wardrobe and found myself in a crisis as most of the people can relate I had nothing to wear. So I went to my sister's room this is one of the very few benefits of having a sibling. While I was looking for something to wear, I found a bottle of perfume so I thought I would try it and God! It smelled like one of those sprays that are for cockroaches and that smelled so familiar. It made me recall something that I have never shared with anyone. Something I was not proud of. Few days ago ...it wasn't the first time I thought about killing myself and you might think it would have been some time during my teenage years but no it was when I was in 4th-5th standard. Growing up my mom always used to tell me that I had very bad luck and it was because of my bad luck that my dad passed away and I made him suffer the three years he was around because I would cry all day and wouldn't let him sleep at night, she still says that sometimes but it doesn't hurt that much now.

One night I had a fight with my mom (when I was in 4ᵗʰ or 5ᵗʰ) and she said the same thing and at that time I got convinced that it was true. So while my mom was sleeping, I was crying in a corner and it suddenly hit me that if I just died, I wouldn't be bad luck. So I started to look around and I found that spray. I was a kid, I didn't think that it may not kill me and may just have some harmful after effects. So I was going to ingest it because I wanted my mom to know how much she hurt me and I wanted her to regret (yes I know that's evil and i did think that). And I even wrote a note that probably no one would understand because of how terrible my handwriting was. After that I just sprayed it in the cap of the bottle and I ingested it. It didn't do anything; I just threw up after a while and the next day too. My stomach was hurting so bad but I refused to go to the doctor because I was scared that everyone was going to find out. I have never told this to anyone. I didn't know if anyone was going to understand. While my mother didn't mean any of those words but they kept messing with my mind and that feeling of guilt was unknown to me before that. Guilt is like a parasite, it keeps feeding on you until it is too late and you can no longer remove that parasite without hurting yourself

At that time what I regretted the most was spraying that perfume on my wrist, its smell won't go away .As I went back to my room and saw all the mess that was still there. The memories that where lying on the floor and the things that were still misplaced, I felt like the space around me was shrinking. I ended up with a headache. It started from the left side of my head and it felt like something was penetrating into my head. Those were the memories that I chose to recall today. I found myself in the middle of nowhere. Those memories came like tides in the sea-rising and falling with every breath as a gasped for air. The chaos had imprisoned me. It was choking my breath. It felt like I was falling deeper and deeper into something that had no end. Suddenly my mother came in. It felt like my body was going to shrink so tight that my soul would escape she came to me and hugged me in such a way that she could hear my heart, beating faster and faster. She looked into my restless eyes and kissed my forehead and she asked "are you fine? You look sad". My lips didn't move but my eyes could clearly say that I didn't want to be alone at that time. "Let me wait here till you're ready" she said. I suddenly didn't feel anything. I was empty and numb. I held myself together and got up'

Getting ready to meet my friends, instead of being happy and excited, I was caught by nervousness for no reason. Somehow I made it to my friend's house. We saw each other after three long months. So we hugged each other tight. One by one all of my friends arrived. Like all the other girls we started gossiping. I had been dying to see my friends but at that time their voices felt like unwanted noises that were teasing my mind. I laughed with them at the silliest things while my heart ached. All of my friends were so happy to see each other but I was empty. I was lost in my own thoughts.

After we were all caught up with all the current drama in our life, it was time to talk reminisce the beautiful memories of our childhood. Two of our friends were cousins and they had always done everything together and it was always fun to hear their stories. This time they started to talk some funny incident that happened in their vacation.

Vacations used to be so exiting for all the kids. You got to spend time at your maternal home with your cousins and all. For others the vacations were for three months, mine was for four years. We spent four years at Naanu's house. My friends would always say "you are so lucky. You have so much time to spend at your maternal home. You must enjoy it a lot, right? They would me to share stories about how I spent my time there. It was very pretty cool for them. But only I knew the real story.

I had two maternal uncles. The elder one was a shopkeeper and the younger one was a lecturer. My Naanu would come home after days. My elder Maamu used to take care of me and family. He wouldn't let anyone know about his struggles. My younger Maamu had no knowledge about the family matters. He was the youngest of all the siblings that's why he was pampered a lot.

It was a cold winter night; I was watching a movie named "Johnny mera naam" with my Maamu. I had no idea what was going on in the movie. There were some people beating up a guy and asking him "who are you? What is your name? "I had no idea what was going on in the movie. So I kept asking Maamu" what is his name?? "

"Jonny" he replied

I asked "why are they asking him again and again? Why would people beat up someone to know his name?" I asked these questions so many times that Maamu got angry and he said "I'm never going to watch a movie with you again" I didn't know he really meant it.

I said "I'm not going to leave you alone to watch a movie".

He replied "tomorrow you're going to your uncle's house, who is going to stop me from watching a movie alone?"

I thought for a while and said "that would be the last time you that you watched a movie alone" and Maamu smiled. In the meantime, my cousin came with a guest list and his wedding invitations which were not filled yet. I was watching them as they were filling up the invitation cards and discussing about the wedding. My Maamu was telling him not to worry about anything because he would take care of everything on the wedding. Like most of the Kashmiri men, my cousin didn't want the women to sing on his wedding and he told Maamu "they are only going to listen to you", you'll have to tell them not to sing"

Maamu, who too didn't like women singing on weddings, came up with an unexpected answer "what's wrong with it? It is there way of expressing their happiness, let them do it", who knew no one was actually going to sing.

The next day I went to my uncle's house. I was overwhelmed to see my cousin, who had come home after a long time but I was also thinking "Maamu would be watching movies alone, he'll be enjoying without me". After a long day of listening to Aapi's stories and went to sleep. I woke up in the middle of night, my whole body was shaking, my heart was beating faster and I called my cousin. "Aapi I'm scared" I whispered

She asked me what I was scared of and I said "something awful is going to happen". She comforted me by saying "calm down, it was just a dream".

The next day my Naanu came early in the morning, I had just waked up and I asked him "can't I come later?"

"My child! It's already too late" he replied.

I got into the car and started to ask Naanu "what happened?".

He was silent, or frozen I should rather say. An army officer stopped us on the way as there had been a curfew since 9th of February, 2013. The officer asked "where are you going?" Naanu replied, coverings his eyes with his hand "we have to attend a funeral. Our relative passed away".

Numerous thoughts came in my mind at that time. My whole body started shaking, my heart was beating faster and I couldn't breathe properly, I was scared. When we reached at Naanu's house, I saw some men crying outside the gate. I stepped out of the car, my legs were shaking. I heard someone screaming "the fire has broken out, we are ruined and everything has turned into ashes". All the people around me were crying. I was numb and I had no idea what was going on. My eyes were looking for my super hero-my mom. For me she was the strongest person I ever knew. She had lost her mother at 7. Her father would come home after months. At this age she took the responsibility of her siblings and looked after them like their mother would do. She gave half of her life to her siblings and now was the time for her other half. She married to the kindest and the most helpful man. He always helped the needy ones. People would consider him as an angel. That was the reward for my mother's sacrifices but that too didn't last long. She lost her husband after 5 years of her marriage and was with two daughters. She still had hopes, her brother was her strength.

I found my super hero surrounded by many people, wiping her tears. They could only see the tears that rushed from her eyes but I could feel her heart weeping. I was trying to approach her and some pulled me out of the crowd and took me inside. I was left alone there. I heard a phone ringing in the store room. I picked up the phone, it was a woman who was crying and she asked me "where is your Maamu?

Someone took the phone from my hand and he said "it is Farooq Ahmed who passed away, hello! Hello! Can you hear me?"

Farooq Ahmed was my Maamu. My whole body started

shaking, my heart was shattered and I wanted someone to tell me "calm down, it's just a dream". I didn't believe it. As soon as I tried to go out, my Maami came with a one month old baby crying in her arms. They took the baby inside and his elder brother Fahad who was just 6 years old was trying to comfort him. They came inside with the baby. I was looking at him as he was crying. I couldn't take my eyes off him. It was heart wrenching to see that innocent face. I used to complain to God "why did you take my father? I had only 3 years to spend with him" but when I saw that one month old baby whom his father lifted only once in his arms, I forgot all my complaints. Meanwhile, my uncle came in. He took me in his arms and said "this will be the last time you see your Maamu" but I refused.

"My child, you have to face this. You won't be able to see him again" after hearing this I say a word. He took me see my Maamu. I couldn't look and him for more than a few seconds and I closed my eyes.

My Naanu told me "Fahad is waiting for you in his room. He doesn't know anything. You have to take care of him. Make sure you don't cry in front of him" I went to Fahad and the moment he saw me, he hugged me tight and said "I missed you a lot. Come let's watch a movie. I don't like to watch TV alone...."

At that time my younger Maamu needed emotional support. So, my mom decided to stay with him until he recovers from the loss. My Naanu took over the shop. With time everything was back on the track but the wounds were still fresh. Nobody could recover from that loss but for each other's happiness, everyone used to pretend that everything was fine. I always used to complain to God "why do you take away everyone who could take care of me?" I was emotionally broken down. But when a looked at my mother, the way she concealed her scares gave me courage. She never complained to God. She didn't care about what society thought of her. The society wouldn't see her scares. People would still criticize her for stays too long at her maternal home. There were some people who had sympathy for us. But the way they used to show it was enough for someone to lose belief in God.

"Why doesn't God show pity on your daughters? They lost father in such a young age. What was their fault? They had their Maamu to take care of them but that too didn't last long". That's all they would say. But mother never lost hope. She used to tell people that she was our father and we didn't need anyone else. Her positivity gave us strength. Years passed and I started to accept that God has planned something better for us. Things become easier when start accept the pain instead of trying to forget it. Life keeps going on. Experiences that break you are the ones that make. You get up stronger every time you fall.

The pain didn't stop there. While I was healing, life took another ugly turn. It was January 2016, my Naanu was hospitalized. Mama was with him. So, I was taken to my uncle's house. This was reminding me of something very painful. But I was still trying to be positive. I spent that night at my uncle's house, restlessly. I was recalling all the moments I spent with my Naanu.

I don't know how but he could read my heart. He would just look into my eyes and he would see my pain. When I was a kid, he used make me sit on his shoulders and took me for a walk. As kid he appeared to me like Santa Claus, because he had this long white beard. I used to comb his beard. I even used to braid it.

While thinking of him, my heart was beating faster, tears rolled off my cheeks and I was still smiling. I fell asleep while crying. Next day my aunt woke me up in the morning and told me that Naanu was in a critical condition. I immediately got up, made waddu and started to offer namaz. I was praying to God to ease his pain. My uncle came to me and hugged me tight. He looked into my eyes and said "have faith in God. Everything happens for a reason. Your Naanu was in pain and now his pain is relieved. Hurry up! We need to go".

I just wiped my tears and got into the car. As soon as we reached there, I was told to go inside. The environment there didn't look like Naanu had come home, fully recovered from the pain. I didn't know anything worse could happen. This time I was only given clues. Nobody said that Naanu passed away. Maybe that thought I would guess it as I had got used to these kinds of incidents. I was in a shock. The people around me were telling me to cry it out. But I didn't cry. This time I went on my own to see my Naanu for the last time and to bid him goodbye. I went to him, my hands were shaking and for the last time a combed his beard. As I was drowning deep inside my thoughts, I heard someone calling me, it was my friend and realized I had completely zoned out. I had no idea what they were talking about. They kept asking me but I didn't say a word. I knew that no one was going to understand. It was better for me to remain a mystery to the world. Whenever I tried to share my pain with people, they would part themselves from me and make me realize that I was meant to be alone. With a tired soul, a chaotic mind and tears in my eyes, I went home. As I went into my room, I saw that mess I had made in my room and I realized this is something that I started and at the end of the day I am the only one who would have to finish it. So I told myself that I had to it. So I picked up all the stuff from the ground. The last few things that were left were the paperweight that my Maamu gave me and my cousin (his son) and we would always fight over it even though we didn't that it was. After Maamu's death, I begged my cousin to let me keep that paperweight .and there was this watch that naanu once dropped in the kaangri, the day he died, someone was putting his stuff away and that watch fell out of this pocket of his pheran . I could have kept any of his belonging but I don't know why I wanted to keep that watch

The last thing in that box was an old diary in which I used to write my poems. It reminded me of how I first started writing

It was an ordinary afternoon in Kashmir. Some kilometers away from my home, there was an encounter going on. I was sitting in the backyard of my house. I had my sketch book with me; I thought I'd draw something. I could see the smoke at a distance. I could hear the bullets that were hitting someone's home. Someone who had that house with his blood and sweat and someone who spent his childhood there would have been seeing their memories and efforts turning into smoke. I knew that this is the future of all Kashmiris. All of would have to face this one day. I couldn't speak about it. That's when I felt the need to write that's when I started to write and once you enter the world of observing and writing, there is no turning back. I think being able to write is the best thing that has ever happened to me. during the initial phase of my writing, I would write poems with difficult words and no hidden meanings, I would just write the truth but as I grew up I realized that poetry was all about hoe convincingly you could lie I believe that poetry is just some beautiful lies that are too strong to not believe in. then I began t*o see writing in a different way and I realized that it was not about making people understand something, it was about making them feel something, something that you didn't give them but something they already had. There are always some personal experiences that inspire a writer. For me writing felt like freshening up old wounds and making them bleed on paper. Writing felt like untangling all my chaos. "Chaos" I don't know why this word has been my favorite, you might think it's just a fancy word for "confusion" and it's such a simple word if you think about it. But for me it was more than just that. Someone who was once close to me hated that word because I would use that word too often in my writing when I felt like no one would understand me although they wanted to understand me. That's when it hit me, that word of perfect for me. That's when I knew if I ever wrote about my life id name it chaos.

It is now 9PM and I already want to go bed. This is not normal for me, I was an insomniac but these few weeks I had been sleeping for more than 10 hours. I don't know if you can call that sleep, my body would just shut down at a point and it felt like my brain was too tired to make my body work. Weeks ago I would give anything to sleep for more than 4 hours. These weeks have been tough for me. It feels like a part of me is missing, very important part. The part of me which had a desire to live life to its fullest. I haven't done anything productive in days. I haven't studied, I haven't eaten properly not on purpose but I just didn't feel the desire to eat. All I did these days was sleeping to avoid everything. There is no such problem in the world that has no solution, if only I knew what the problem was. My heart had been on fire and there was no amount of tears which could put it off. I had been feeling like a loser and I was tired of pretending to fit in. there was no incident that happened that would have triggered this. I would pray every night that I don't wake up next morning and I prayed that everyone would forget who I was. When I prayed for many days and it didn't get answered, I even thought of doing it myself. I don't know if I actually wanted that or not. I felt like I there was no hope to live there was some kind of guilt that I had, I had this fear of losing everything I have, I was scared to be left alone by everyone so one by one I pushed everyone away so that they don't get a chance to leave me. Because it was all in my head, no could understand. I didn't try to make anyone understand because no one made me feel like they wanted to know. Eventually they did leave and I ended up here. Each night I had been distracting myself so I wouldn't cry. At moments my heart would ache and my legs would shake so much that I could stand up, in that moment I felt very close to death. But that's the only moment when I feel

But tonight I want to see how much pain is buried inside of me. I have decided that I won't stop myself from crying tonight. I want to let all of it out so that I never cry about it again.

After a point you crying eventually when there are no more tears left but right now I have completely drained myself, physically and emotionally. Now I really need some sleep. As I am getting into bed, I can feel something crawling on neck. There it is! How did I forget about that spider!

I still don't know if I'm going to wake up tomorrow but I want to be remembered.......

"So remember me when you look at the moon,
How it goes unnoticed on the nights it's healing,
How everyone loves it when it's full or about to vanish.
So remember me when you look at art,
Because I was never meant to be understood by everyone,
I was meant to be watched at a distance
And never to be touched.
So remember me when you look at the sunset,
How it makes you believe some endings are worth it."

Dear reader,

I'm glad you made it till the last page. I am grateful that you found my worth reading. I am glad to be able share my experiences with you. This book is just the beginning. I have a lot more to share. I hope I get a chance.